BEYOND THE VEIL

STORIES OF THE PARANORMAL

THE TOWER
Pat Marsden

CHAPTER ONE

Amanda tossed her green shawl in the general direction of the hall tree, dropped her mail, and the evening paper on the telephone table, with just a quick glance in the hall mirror, on the way into the kitchen. I'm not a fan of bright colors, but after the scandal, and diatribe I endured in The Village, going incognito, and forgoing my favorite black shawl in favor of the green, and cutting my hair appeared my best option. *The shorter hair is convenient, but I don't even recognize myself. My long hair did give me so many more ways that I could do it than this short bob does. However, the short cut is flattering and easy to take care of.*

"A cup of tea is what I chiefly need." She said to Charlie, kicking off her shoes, and turning on the burner under the teakettle all at the same time. Amanda didn't believe in wasting time, and seldom did one thing when she could do two.

"Although, what I'm saving all this time, for now, I don't know." She said addressing Charlie again. The big orange cat didn't say anything. He just blinked at her with his golden eyes and yawned sleepily, exposing his pink tongue, and sharp, white teeth. He may be the laziest cat in all creation, or at least a close second, but he was dear to her, and she loved him very much. "I like talking with you Charlie; it is nice to have someone listen without judgment."

He was number one cat, named after a favorite uncle, long deceased, and he, and Amanda kept house together for four years before Becky and Jo turned up on the doorstep one rainy fall night about a year ago. They were so tiny, and sopping wet, that they fairly tumbled over each other getting to the warmth of the fireplace, and the dish of milk she set down for them.

Charlie scrutinized each one, and then held them down, and unceremoniously washed them from stem to stern, one after the other. Since then they had been one happy family. It seemed the only time Charlie wasn't lazy was when he was washing or playing with the kittens.

She named the new arrivals after characters in her favorite books. Becky was named after Tom Sawyer's girlfriend because she was such a sweetheart and all blonde fluff. Jo, a real tomboy, all black and white, so she was named after Jo March in Little Women. The two girls and Charlie became her family, and in some ways, her closest friends. *Not to say that I lack 'people friends. Lord no, there were lots of those, but in many ways, her 'people friends were not as close.' I'm well different.* She thought.

"Let's see, shall I have spice or herb tea? Ah, almond, I think." Charlie was indifferent; he had gone back to sleep. If it wasn't their mealtime, play time, or cuddle time, he just wasn't all that interested in what she drank.

After pouring the boiling water into the teapot, dropping two tea bags in, she gave it time to seep, as she fed the cats, and made herself a light supper of sliced chicken, between two pieces of homemade bread, no mayonnaise of course, she hated mayonnaise, and added a few cookies on the plate; extras of course, for the cats. They did have a sweet tooth.

CHAPTER TWO

Tea prepared, the cats fed, and herself changed into her old, comfortable robe, and fuzzy slippers, Amanda carried her supper tray into her sitting room, set it down, and tossed a match into the fire she had laid out that morning. "Gee! It's nice to be home!" She stated after settling down into her favorite chair.

Charlie and the girls strolled in past the fire and took up their accustomed places. *Funny how much cats were like people, except of course they didn't talk at you nonstop.* Each had a favorite spot, just like I always sit in this same chair, and feel vaguely uncomfortable if an unsuspecting guest chose it. *Was it a territorial thing? Or did certain spots acquire the aura of their usual occupants?*

I'm not going to think about auras or any such things tonight. It has been a long, long day, and I am bone tired. Besides, it brings back too many memories, and it lets the outside world in too. "I sure wish I didn't have the curse of picking up other people's thoughts and emotions.

Now you know old girl if you don't get up, and do something about that telephone, it's going to ring, and there'll go your peaceful evening at home." She said to herself, but not before finishing her sandwich — *no sense in getting up twice.*

After silencing the bell, and turning on her answering machine, she gathered up her mail and the evening paper. "All the bills and the junk mail can wait till tomorrow. Don't you think Charlie? I can look through them at breakfast. It's just like me to never throw a thing away without looking through, or at least glancing at it. You never know when something interesting will show up. Call it an insatiable curiosity." She always said to anyone who questioned her. *Maybe it went with the territory, so to speak – which came first, the chicken or the egg?* "Come on, not tonight." She scolded herself.

Jo howled at the door; she wanted to go out. *It is unusual; most nights they are all content to use the litter box after dark.*

"Oh dear, I hope she doesn't have a boyfriend. Kittens I don't need."

CHAPTER THREE

Standing on her front stoop, waiting for Jo, she thought. It is a lovely evening. Just a slight chill in the air that brings a hint of an early fall, but there was only a gentle breeze, and a full moon to round out the picture. Once again, Amanda congratulated herself on her good fortune in moving to such a pleasant little town. *How aptly named, Pleasantville, and yes, the town lived up to its name all right. The decision to move hadn't been an easy one, and most of her city friends thought she had gone bonkers, but it had worked out well. Of course, there were drawbacks; nothing in life is ever one hundred percent perfect, but all-in-all, it was the right decision.*

"Sometimes I wish Ken and Barbara were here and could drop in when things got sticky, and I miss the bunch down at the Village Inn." *But life had gotten much too hectic, too busy, and way too public after that last affair. That one was a bit of a horror, what with me leading the cops to the body, and having to explain how I knew it would be there. After that, I had to pick out the perp from the line-up. Since I hadn't seen him, except in a vision, it had every crackpot journalist, crazy cult member, and even those interested in finding a family member, knowing their future coming out of the woodwork. But the worst was the friends and family members of the murder after me, and what a stink the papers made of it. Goodness knows why they wouldn't leave me alone. It got to the point where even Dr. Evens thought I should get away for a bit, at least till things died down, but would they?*

"Hah! I bet they never thought – any of them – that I'd stay away for good! Where is Jo? Drat, that cat.' Amanda said as she turned to go in.

'I'll just let her stay out and see how she likes them apples!" But here came Joe, trotting up like nothing in the world was the matter. *Maybe there isn't a boyfriend. Perhaps, it's just the night and the full moon? I need to get those two in for their operations. Kittens do not fit into my plans.*

Amanda pushed the door closed and turned off the porch light. In her neighborhood, a lighted porch is an invitation for anyone just to drop in, and she didn't want company tonight. Today had been something else. *If I'm honest with myself, the entire week had been way too busy for my taste. Funny how things had worked out. When I bought this house, I envisioned days of sleeping late, and little social contacts, but it had turned out just the opposite. I'm just as busy — maybe even more so — than I when I lived in the city. The only difference is that it is now the fun and games type of busy. There isn't the pressure, and I do not*

want or need all the publicity. Nor do I have all the
people wanting to know their future, or heaven
forbid the friends of the murder looking for her,
and let's not forget that awful cult. She shuddered
just thinking about it.

"Boy, those last weeks before she left were
bad. I really wish I wasn't born with the so-called
gift of sight. Oh well, shake it off. Right guys?" She
asked the cats.

CHAPTER FOUR

Here in her little home in her small town, she could even turn off her telephone without feeling guilty. *Hell, she hadn't yet played back the day's messages! Let them wait till morning; Tonight, is my night to just loaf. Only why am I so tired? Maybe I am coming down with something. Flu? No, it must be I need some vitamins or a bit more rest.*

Sinking back into her comfortable chair, she poured another cup of tea. "Charlie, buying this electric trivet was one of my more intelligent purchases. Remember how it was either cold tea, or I was always jumping up to warm up the pot?" Charlie lay on the braided rug, his front paws folded under him, and eyes on her, as if he were listening intently to her every word. Becky, as usual, chose the cricket chair near the fireplace, and Jo curled up in her usual spot underneath Becky's chair. The fire crackled, and the cats purred. It was her idea of peaceful.

Darn! Why do I feel so tired? No, it's more like a heavy weight sitting on my chest. Maybe, I am coming down with something. Well, if I'm getting sick, I'd better look at the mail first.

Nothing much – a couple of 'thank you's,' an invitation to a baby shower, and one to a birthday party. The Garden Club wanted her to speak, a freebie, of course, a letter from her sister, and a crudely printed envelope, that was obviously from a child. Though why a child would write to her, she didn't know.

"I'll read Melanie's first, the one from the child can wait." Her sister had married well, and once widowed she moved into a Florida condominium, where she spent countless hours playing bridge, basking in the sun, and chasing eligible widowers. Melanie never had much to say that interested Amanda. The bulk of her correspondence consisted of various ploys designed to get Amanda to join her in Florida, and 'live the good life.'

"I suppose I really should take a couple of weeks and spend some time with her. Perhaps this winter would be a good time? Nah, I'll never leave you three, besides I don't like Florida, I detest bridge, and the sun makes my skin break out, and last-but-not-least I'd be bored silly and miss you three. Still, I do feel guilty sometimes.

Damn! Why do I let people get to me?" Amanda stated.

Finally, she picked up the last letter. It was just a cheap, brown envelope with her name and address hand-printed on it, in crayon, with a local postmark. Suddenly, she didn't want to open it. Something was very wrong. Slowly she slit the envelope and looked at its contents. No child sent this!!!! There was no note or any word of explanation. The only thing in the envelope was one of the Tarot cards – one of the trumps – the Major Arcana. It was the Struck Tower. Now she knew why she felt so tired and weighted down.

Amanda looked at the cats. "Here we go again. The question is, does it mean destruction, or liberation, and who do you think has found me?" She whispered.

JANE DOE
A Paranormal Christmas Story
Patricia Moran

PROLOGUE

Sliding notes of silver filled Gillian's ears just before she heard what sounded like a door slam. After that, she heard the breeze blowing through the branches of the white pine above her, where she lay in a nest of pine needles and leaves. Her long red hair flowed nearly to her feet helping to keep the chill from her body. The bird's song, and she the sound of scampering feet climbing down from the tree filled her ears.

Rough wet noses touched her, and her hand reached up to pet the black fur of the bear cubs. Her thoughts reached out to them and asked. "Where is your momma little ones?" At first, she heard nothing back, as they nuzzled her, cuddling into her and she felt their hunger. "Has she gone to eat?" Gillian tried again.

"Yes!" Was the only answer she received from the two, as they cuddled closer for warmth.

"It is chilly out here, isn't it? Is this your nest?" She said with her mind. It was what came naturally to her. So seldom did she speak out loud, it wasn't needed with her people. *Who are my people? Where am I? Who am I?*

Only the warmth of the cubs, the clean smell of them, and for a while the feeling of belonging answered her.

All too soon the cubs grew stiff next to her. She smelled the musky scent of the wolves. Easy little ones, it will be okay, she said disentangling herself from them.

The wolf smell became stronger as she knelt, sending out thoughts of calmness and love toward them. Gillian's awareness of all that was around her, noticed the cubs had fled back up the tree as she knelt on the ground, ready to face the wolves.

And they came toward her, quietly until the circled her. First one then another came forward and sniffed her, as her mind reached out to talk to them. Soothing them, calming them. "These little ones aren't for you.' She thought as she stroked their roughened fur. 'You've been rolling in stinky stuff, haven't you?"

She continued to pet each of them, and they chirped happily, though when she stopped petting one, it whined I'm hungry whine until she petted it again. Gillian sensed the bear cubs fear and whispered a calming toward them while sending the wolves off in another direction for breakfast.

"I can't stay here as much as I'd like to little ones." She said as she stood up. Clothed only in what God had given her, Gillian gave each little cub a pat and began walking.

As she moved further away from the cubs toward the lights and buildings in the distance, Gillian became tired, and cold, she thought again. *Who am I, where am I, why am I so cold?*

CHAPTER ONE

Jane sat back on the old sofa, sinking into the hollows between the broken springs. It had been an effort to climb the four flights of rickety stairs to her small attic room. She felt the aching weariness creep up her legs, her hips, all the way to her head, even her long red hair hurt today.

She was just too tired tonight to take off her coat, she sat, almost in a trance, staring int the nothingness on the opposite wall.

Once long ago, a mirror had hung there, but the pain of seeing nothing but her own face day after day had caused her to take it down. The mirror now stood with its back to the wall near the closet door, leaving only a faded rectangle where it had been.

Downstairs she heard the holiday party, people talking and laughing. Several voices were singing 'Silent Night' slightly off-key. Someone else tuned up a guitar and began a bawdy version of 'Rudolph the Red-Nosed Reindeer.' The notes, the singing, the shrill voices of the women and the loud voices of the men, rose and swirled about her like living things; a jangled cacophony of discordance until her mind screamed in agony for silence. Even though they were Christmas songs, the horrible noise was nearly as bad as when they had a party and played Metallica, it jarred her to her bones.

With a wave of her hand, the gas stove lit under the teakettle. At least here I don't have to be careful and can do what comes naturally to me. Though even here I must not use those abilities that it seems others don't have for fear that I will become careless when out in the world.

She always felt alone and somehow different, at least since she had wandered into this town.

The doctors at the charity hospital assured her that once her memory returned the strangeness would disappear, but after nine years she had lost hope.

The police had found her unconscious in an alley nothing but her long red hair covered her nakedness. She appeared unharmed, except for a large bump on her head, but had absolutely nothing on her to identify her by. Her fingerprints were not in the system, nor did anyone step forward to claim her, as the weeks turned to months even the police lost interest and stopped trying to trace her. Everyone lost interest, even she began to lose interest, though she loved to remember what she could.

CHAPTER TWO

It was only at Christmas that a certain magic and sparkle in the air brought to her consciousness the knowledge that once, long ago, things had been different. Fleeting impressions of another time, another place, and people who were like her teased at the corners of her mind. With those memories' brief flashes of air like crystal and golden light, the sweet aromas, of things she couldn't place, and a glimpse of a man filled her senses. Then the loneliness became unbearable and she longed for death.

Last year she had tried to break the spell by joining the party downstairs, but the ribaldry, the incongruity of celebrating the Baby's birthday with a drunken party, had driven her in tears to her room. This year they hadn't asked her, nor would she have gone if they had.

The party downstairs subsided momentarily, and she could hear the bells on the Cathedral pealing out the Christmas story. It was nearly midnight. Sputtering and hissing, the teakettle boiled over the hot plate, breaking into her reverie. Turning it off, she sat down heavily, her head resting on the back of the faded sofa, tears sliding down her cheeks.

"Oh Lord, I want to go home, wherever home is for me. Please, Lord, I want to go home."

A hush came over the room. The sounds of the outside world faded where the mirror had once hung, the wall simply melted away. As if in a dream, he stood there, bathed in shimmering golden light. He held out his arms and called her by a name she had forgotten, and suddenly she remembered, it all became clear.

BEYOND THE VEIL

The Cathedral bells clamored wildly, and their exaltation filled the tiny, shabby room, as she stepped into the shimmering, golden radiance.

The newspapers made quite a thing of it. The police probed and questioned. The public feasted its voracious appetite for the bizarre, but the questions remained unanswered.

The woman they called Jane had been seen going into her room and she did not come out, nor was she ever seen again. Her room was as it had been, except for a little pile of discarded clothing on the floor and a blossom of some unknown flower that protruded from the wall.

Gillian had gone home, she just needed to ask.

MISS TOFTE
Patricia Moran & Marta Moran Bishop

CHAPTER ONE

Who I am is not pertinent to this story, in fact, I'd rather not say and I'm sure you will understand after reading further.

I was a beginning typist the day I first met Miss Tofte at the Apex Insurance Company. Even then I thought she was a little strange, I soon learned that mentioning this was definitely off-limits. I mean, Lillian Tofte had been at the company so long she was practically an institution.

It was all right to criticize the company president if you felt like it, but never Miss Tofte. After all presidents, supervisors, and executives came and went, but Lillian Tofte stayed. As far as anyone knew she had been there forever, or so it seemed, for no one knew how long she had been with the company. She started years before any proper records were kept, and a personnel department hadn't even been dreamed of at the time. Maybe, she herself knew, but somehow you didn't dare ask her. It was kind of like asking someone's age, you know, strictly personal.

As far as age went, Miss Tofte, for no one called her Lillian was ageless, in an ancient and very, very old sort of way. When I first went to work there, she seemed to me to be in her late sixties. After my ten-year anniversary with the company, I had gotten older, just as everyone else had, but not Miss Tofte. She was the same, somewhere in her late sixties. What's more, I learned from talking to one of the senior employees, Miss Tofte looked the same as long as she could remember.

She was a small, thin woman and appeared gray. I mean really gray! Her hair and eyes were gray, and even her skin seemed a bit gray. What's more, she wore gray clothes. All her clothes were gray, some darker, some lighter, but all of them some shade of gray. Why she even acted gray, if characters can be said to have a color. She was just a slow-moving gray little blob and she crept. The few times she left the file room, she practically hugged the walls, blending into those gray walls.

Miss Tofte had a whispery, feathery little voice when she spoke, which she did rarely. Usually, she'd just listen to you, with her head to one side and then nod, or shake her head, indicating a yes or no. I guess her voice had all but disappeared from lack of use. Not her mind though, she was sharp as a tack. It was just that she didn't go in for verbal communication. She wrote memos, thousands of memos. Hardly a day would go by

when you didn't get a memo from Miss Tofte.

They were all about the same thing, her files.

CHAPTER TWO

You see, Miss Tofte was in sole charge of the files, they were her children. Once, long ago they had tried to give her an assistant, but she got so upset that the company just let her continue on her own. So, there she was day in and day out all alone in her file department. Miss Tofte re-arranged, re-dated, moved them up or down, checked files in and checked them out. She relabeled, reorganized, and re-glued her precious file children, and she wrote memos to everyone about them.

If you needed a file, you were given a time limit on a check out just like in a library. Even the president of the company had to check a file back in and out again if he still needed it for a longer period. No one was exempt. I will say that we had the best-kept file section of any I'd ever heard of, but it all was carried to the extreme if you know what I mean. It was just as though the company had no other purpose than to provide the room for the file section. As far as Miss Tofte was concerned, they were the be-all and end-all to life. You could find her there puttering around before anyone else every morning and even if you worked late at night, she'd still be there opening and shutting file drawers when you left. As far as I knew she slept in a file drawer!

Behind her filing section, Miss Tofte had a tiny little washroom and a hot plate, so during the day she never left her department. As I intimated if she left at night no one knew it. Personnel had no home address or next of kin for her, she did not mix socially or any other way with anyone at work and never mentioned anything outside of the file department.

I guess when they had first put in a personnel department, someone had requested information from her, but she carried so much weight with the old president she got away with ignoring them.

Everyone in the company was so used to her after all those years, no one bothered her for any reason, not even for a home address, or next of kin. At any rate, she had her own rules and she gave me an eerie feeling.

I found myself wondering if she had been born out of the files or they were born together. At any rate, the files and Miss Tofte were inextricably tied up with each other. I tell you it was weird!

CHAPTER THREE

If it had been anybody else, I would have felt kind of sad about it, I mean, a little old lady with no life other than the file department. But with Miss Tofte, you had an altogether different feeling. This was the way she liked it, make no mistake, this was her choice.

Anyway, I guess I have pretty well established that to all appearances Miss Tofte had always and was always in the files, and she gave every indication of going on this same way forever. She probably would have too if something had not happened to change her world.

CHAPTER FOUR

It happened right around my tenth anniversary when the rumors began about the merger. Oh, rumors like these had been around before and most of us older employees didn't pay much attention to them, but this one was different.

Bright and early one morning in January each of us received an official notice from the President. The rumors were true. Our company was merging with a large Eastern Insurance Combine and we were all being notified about our status. Some folks were being terminated, some were going on as usual with the new company, and some people were given the option to go with the new company in a different capacity. As you can well imagine there wasn't a great deal of work accomplished that day. People were gathered in little groups all over the office talking about the merger and what it would mean to them.

I had already decided that I'd move to a new job. I'd been thinking about it for some time anyway and this was as good a time as any to make the change. After all, if I stayed here for many more years, heaven forbid I might end up like Miss Tofte.

Good Lord! We had all forgotten Miss Tofte. Of course, the filing department would be different and probably run differently as well. Especially since the Combine had everything computerized. What would happen to Miss Tofte?

Gradually this line of thought worked its way through the entire office and people began to turn and glance uneasily toward the filing department. Miss Tofte and her dedication to the files was a matter of general knowledge. I mean, she was so wrapped up in them it was impossible

to think of her in any other connection.

CHAPTER FIVE

A few of us suddenly decided we had urgent business in the filing section. Miss Tofte was busily arranging a cabinet and took little notice of us until one girl actually reached out and opened a file drawer. Instantly she was upon us, apparently her same old self, and gave no indication of any forthcoming change. I started to ask her if she had heard about the merger, but something in her manner cut me off. As I have said, she was not the type of person you had idle chatter with. She never indulged in office gossip and seemed totally unaware of us except as we related to her precious files. No one else said anything and it was impossible to guess if she knew about the merger or not.

The next morning Joe, one of the janitors, told us he had found the official notice crumpled in her wastebasket. So, Miss Tofte had known and had decided to ignore the entire thing, just as she ignored the Personnel Department's requests for information so very long ago.

In February we learned that filing was one of the first to go. The entire department would be moved to a new location, and a new system installed. After micro-filming all our files, the files would be destroyed except those current and pertinent to the new company. Obviously, there would be no place for Miss Tofte; she was being put out to pasture, despite this Miss Tofte was conducting business as usual. There had not been the least change in her attitude or her routine. I wondered what was going to happen on April 1st when the new company moved in and the old Insurance company was no more.

CHAPTER SIX

Actually, none of us had much time to think about anything with all the commotion going on around us. It had been determined that not one working day would be lost, so we scurried about trying to close out as much as possible and transfer what was left.

Meanwhile, men moved partitions and even walls, shoved file cabinets around and replaced signs. Of course, as the month wore on, desks and file cabinets were moved in and employees from the new company began working right alongside us. It was a colossal mess.

Throughout the micro-filming, Miss Tofte took everything in stride. After all, it was just checking out files and checking them back in. It was later when a team from management took over and even Miss Tofte was ejected from the file department.

It was queer, but outside of her own domain Miss Tofte looked different. Somehow, she looked tinier than she had before, smaller and grayer. She also seemed much less formidable and appeared not sure of what she was supposed to do.

They put a chair for her next to the door of the file room and someone had to gently force her into it. Actually, I think she was in a state of shock. She seemed not to understand what was going on around her and kept trying to get back into the file room. The team would finish with a cabinet only to find Miss Tofte had crept in behind them as if she was a little gray mouse and began quietly returning all the files to their accustomed drawers. You could just feel the frustration from that team, and finally, the President of the company was called, and he told her gently but firmly that if she entered the file room again, she would be ejected from the building.

This stopped her, and she sank into the chair as though all the life had gone out of her.

Although I felt sorry for her, it did seem as though she was carrying it a little too far. I mean, after all, they were only old files!

They did grant one concession to her; they let her rescue some of the discarded files from the waste boxes. As fast as one was thrown away, within her reach, she would grab it up and place it neatly on the floor beside her. I had no idea what she was going to do with them and neither did anyone else. It really did seem as if she had finally flipped her lid.

Each night at closing time, the team would lock the door and leave, Miss Tofte sitting quietly outside the door with her growing stack of old files. It was all kind of zany and sad.

The thing someone really should have done was to get the company car to take the poor old thing to Bellevue. She had obviously undergone some sort of breakdown. The really odd thing is that Miss Tofte didn't seem any different at all; it was the situation that was different. It was just that poor Miss Tofte couldn't adjust, and I suppose that this is what makes people crazy.

When her world and the real world collided, we realized that Miss Tofte was not only old but, in all probability, completely insane. She had no doubt been that way for years, but in her private world of filing, no one ever noticed. It gave me the creeps. It was bad enough her sitting there collecting old files but to have the rest of the office expected to ignore the entire thing was somehow worse. I mean, what was going to happen when the team was through? Where they just going to leave her sitting there with those stupid files until she died?

It began to appear that is exactly what they were going to do. Right after lunch one day toward the end of March the movers came and took out all the empty cabinets, Miss Tofte's old desk and hot plate, and her empty locker. The janitors came and carried out all the boxes of discarded files to the incinerator, and the carpenters began remodeling the room into a large and sumptuous private office. No one noticed Miss Tofte except me.

Several people went up to her and offered her a ride home that evening, but she just shook her head. I had to work late that night, and when I left the poor old thing was busily cataloging and arranging her salvaged file children.

CHAPTER SEVEN

It's hard to write the last part of this because it doesn't make sense, although nothing about Miss Tofte made much sense, as far as I was concerned. Anyway, I'll tell it like it was, as they say, and everybody will have to make up their own minds about it.

To make a long story short, when I got to work the next morning a little later than usual, everyone was standing around an object in the middle of the room, right next to the door of the former file section. Believe it or not, there stood a very large, very old, very grey filing cabinet. Each of the drawers was neatly labeled, and the contents were obviously those old files Miss Tofte had saved. Largely printed in block letters on the top of the cabinet were the words, "LILLIAN TOFTE – DO NOT TOUCH." Such was the power of Miss

Tofte's personality on us, that no one did. Mis Tofte, herself was nowhere to be seen.

All morning that big, ugly cabinet stood in the middle of the room and dominated the conversation. No one had any idea how it had gotten there, or why she had left it and gone. Actually, it didn't seem to make much difference if she was there or not, because the presence of that file cabinet made us all acutely aware of her. She still dominated the office.

I was the only one to actually see it happen, except for Joe, and he can't be a witness to anything. He never got over it. I didn't want to end up like poor Joe, so I kept my mouth shut when the police came to take him away. The others must have known what happened, but no one wants to believe a thing like that. They'd rather think Joe went crazy moving the file cabinet. Anyway, here is the truth of the matter, just as it happened. You draw your own conclusions.

One of the new people told Joe to get rid of the cabinet, and so he went over to it and put his hand on the top. That's all. I was just sitting there, thinking about Miss Tofte and looking at her poor old filing cabinet, so I saw the entire thing. He just put his hand on it, and as he did the whole thing just crumbled away and appeared on the other wall.

I would have testified for Joe at the sanity hearing if I'd thought it would have done any good, but there would just have been two of us being locked up instead of one. You really couldn't blame the Court though, after all who would believe a story like that?

THE HOUSE THAT HID
Marta Moran Bishop

CHAPTER ONE

It was an odd period in my life, the night I first saw 'The House' and met Mike and his sister Sarah.

You see, I had friends one might call a bit different, though on the surface most of them would appear to be very down to earth types.

D, was a Chicago probation officer, who worked in the court system for the Cook County Sheriff's office. She had long black hair, was ultra-thin, spoke six or seven languages fluently and by all appearances was a normal young woman rising in the sheriff's department. I don't remember how or where I met her, but she introduced me years earlier to Nikki, a musician. Nikki is one of the kindest women I've ever met, with a heart of gold, but if I was feeling a bit of a weirdo, all I had to do was hang around Nikki for a few hours and I'd feel as if I was the most normal person on the planet.

That night D introduced both Nikki and me to Mike and his sister Sarah. Mike was a contractor, you know the type of person who 'if I can't see it or feel it,' it doesn't exist. He was of average height and on the stocky side. But nevertheless, a nice unassuming man, I guess he took Richard Crow's ghost-tour that night because of 'The House.' Because things had changed for Mike after he bought 'The House.'

It was a warm summer night, and the tour was on lake Michigan. It was an uneventful, but fun evening. Perhaps, as Richard said, Ghosts don't usually make as many appearances in warm weather, though I don't know this to be true.

After the tour, Richard invited the five of us to have a late-night bite to eat at the Billy Goat

Tavern, which was frequented by reporters, such as Mike Roko, and many from the crew of SNL. The Billy Goat Tavern was located between the Chicago Sun Times and The Chicago Tribune buildings on the lower level and what one would definitely call a dive. The food was so-so, the atmosphere undeniably-old Chicago, it was built in 1934 and said to be the beginning of the Cubs Curse.

Our conversation revolved around various ghosts that Richard was famous for resurrecting, such as Resurrection Mary as well as many of the most haunted sites in Chicago including the Red Lion Pub and lastly, Mike's house.

Mike had bought 'The House,' about six months earlier. It was built somewhere around the late eighteen hundreds to the early nineteen hundreds.

It was rumored to have been built on top of an old Native American burial ground and once was owned by Al Capone's gang.

CHAPTER TWO

It was white with a porch and a smallish second story and stood on a large lot. I will say that house was in quite a state of disrepair and needed much updating as none had been done since around nineteen hundred and forty or so when Mike bought it and began the renovations.

Sarah was living in the one completed room in the house and though pleasant enough, seemed overly quiet. Not in a shy sort of way, but in a not quite themselves way. It was difficult to pinpoint the oddity of her shyness, but by all accounts, it had begun when she moved into that house.

As with many homes built in that era, the basement was dirt and quite shallow. Too shallow to install today's water heaters and furnace units, so the first thing Mike had to do was dig out a portion of the floor to allow for the taller units. It was during this that he found the lime pit with the remains of human bones.

Of course, he called the police, who determined that the bones were both too old and due to the lime, they were degraded past being able to identify them. But it was suspected their origination was during the years that Al Capone's gang used the house.

It was during the beginning of the renovations that things began to get really crazy in that house. Mike was the sort that laid his tools out in the order he would be using them. But that changed as the tools began moving, he'd reach for one and find another in its place. Frustrated with this, Mike started double checking his layouts, all the while believing he must have laid them out incorrectly. And he began to look at them all the time. At first, he couldn't believe his eyes, when he started to see them moving of their own accord. Though it would only get weirder.

No longer were they moving, but as he worked, they began flying around the room. It was as if some unseen people were playing toss the ball or something similar. It was after that that Mike and Sarah invited the first psychic investigator to the house.

As I had never met either Mike or Sarah before, I was skeptical of his story, though did attempt to keep an open mind. If he hadn't asked us back to the house that night, I would probably have remained skeptical to this day.

CHAPTER THREE

But for what came later at the house. The first thing I noticed during his tour, was the cold spots in the house, though I did put them off to the possibility of drafts. Though it was a warm evening with a little breeze, my mind wanted to believe it was breezes or the result of all the ghost story talk. It wasn't until we finally got to the basement that I knew it was not drafts at all.

There were no windows in the basement, no access to it other than through the main house and it was no colder than any other basement at that time of year. After Mike showed us the box that contained the what remained of the bones, after the cops had removed most of them, Nikki, Mike, and I stood and talked about all that Mike had experienced since he bought that house. As we spoke an icy-cold breeze swept in and around the three of us. I spooked, and just hiked it up the stairs, leaving Mike and Nikki to follow.

It was all I could do to even say goodbye to Mike and Sarah. I barely thanked them and turned to Nikki and said we must go now! I know I was a chicken. I'll tell you honestly, I couldn't help it. There was something or things that meant harm in that house, I could feel them.

I must have appeared very rude, when I hightailed it to Nikki's car, leaving the three of them standing on the porch chatting.

As I sat in the car waiting and watching them on the porch, I noticed the figure upstairs, sitting by the window in Sarah's bedroom, there appeared to be a string like light that somehow joined that old woman to Sarah. I admit it was the strangest thing I had ever seen, and I believed I must be imagining things. I would have put it onto the drink, but I hadn't had a drink that night, nor am I much of a drinker.

I just sat there and watched for a few minutes, until the old woman turned her head, her gaze left Sarah and she looked straight at me. The moment our eyes met, I was filled with such horror, there was something so alien to anything I had ever experienced or even thought of, in her eyes. I felt as if my energy was somehow being tapped, to give her strength, leaving me empty of what was me. I was being robbed of life, and I knew it.

Panic set in. But I managed to pull my gaze away from her and laid my hand on the horn loudly. I didn't think about whether-or-not I would wake the neighbors, cause a commotion or anything except to get Nikki over to the car. I had to leave and NOW. Luckily for me, Nikki did come and quickly, I think I just said, drive. I don't remember much until we were off that street, though I felt the presence of that old woman in the car with us as Nikki drove me home.

I felt the existence of that old woman throughout the night and couldn't shake it. The next morning, I told my mother about the experience, and she wanted to at least drive by the house. After a while I agreed, we would go that afternoon. But first I wanted to do some research to find out what that old woman might be.

It was during my research that I learned of Sentinels; they are a sort of spirit that keeps the most malignant of the other ghosts in a place in check. The problem is they grow old, though it usually takes decades or sometimes centuries for that to happen. From what I read, how long it takes is often decided by how many people they can draw energy from, and she had been alone for a very long time. She needed a replacement, and I feared from what I witnessed she had picked Sarah. By all accounts, before Sarah had moved into that house, she was an outgoing young woman. Not at all like the quiet, introverted woman that I met.

CHAPTER THREE

That afternoon, my mother and I drove to the house, or at least to the place where that house should have been. But it took three or four circles up and down that street before we could find 'that house.' It just wasn't there, the first few times we drove by it.

It only took my mother one minute and one look at the house, before she said to me, "get out of here." It was during the trip home that she said, she believed there was not just a few, but many, many malignant spirits in that house and that it needed an exorcism badly. She wasn't even sure that would work, but without it, people would die, at least Sarah would for sure. Sarah would be trapped in that house forever if it wasn't done. I called Mike and told him what I suspected and gave him my advice on the matter. I believe he thought I was a total nutcase. For whatever reason, I didn't hear back from Mike for nearly a year. It had been late summer when I first saw that house, and it was early the next summer, when I finally received a call from Mike, inviting me to a barbeque.

Apparently, he had finally finished the renovations, and yes, they had had the house exorcised. Not once but by three different groups of people including a Catholic priest.

The day of the barbeque, I re-met, Mike and Sarah. Sarah was a completely changed woman, gone was the quiet, introverted woman, and in her place, I found an average, young woman, interested in men, dating, recipes, the new baby that her sister had. In other words, Sarah was herself again. The house was bright and cheery, without a hint of a ghost of any kind, nor did I feel the presence of that old woman again.

Believe it or not, this is a true story.

THE DEVIL INSIDE
ROMAN NYLE

CHAPTER ONE

Hiding in the shadows, between the building and the streetlamp, Gerard stood quietly, waiting. He had been watching her for two weeks, he knew her schedule, the color of her eyes, and size of her shoes. There wasn't a thing he didn't know about her, at least that is what he believed. She was a feisty, tall redhead, a bit on the plump side, not fat, but what his father would have called pleasingly plump. Just his type too. A little too sure of herself he thought. "I can't wait to take her down a peg or two. He was tall, lanky, and some called him good looking. He could move the muscles in his body in the most unnatural ways or that is what everyone said to him when he was growing up.

"Gerard that is so creepy." He heard so many times in his life. It wasn't his fault that he was born without some of the bones most people had. He could slither around corners almost snakelike as a result and enjoyed terrifying people with it. Actually, as he grew older, he found he absolutely loved to watch the terror in other people's eyes. Especially in the women's eyes. *I'm not sure why I love to terrify women, perhaps it's from watching my father terrify my mother for so many years, that is up until her heart just gave out. I suspect she died from all the gruesome things he saw his father do to her. It became a game for him to watch it, of course it was always from the shadows. That is of course until his father saw him and let him join in the fun.* "You got your *bones from me son. We were born of the Devil the two of us.* "His father told him often enough.

What they did to her was sometimes just cruel, and at other times it was what many would call out right horrible. Still the joy of it grew, and as time went by their secret became their bond. A bond of cruelty and debasement, after all it was as his father would say, "What is a woman for but to bare children, cook, clean, and give whatever pleasure they can to the men folk, and when they are barren, their worth is in watching their pain."

"Ah what days those were. Too bad dad had to up and die on me, but after mother died, he just seemed to shrivel up anyway."

"No more play toys." "Was all he'd say, day after day, hour after hour. I guess it was best that I finally put him out of his misery.' Gerald said to himself. 'Now for miss redhead. I've waited much too long as it is to find just the right one to pick up where dad and I left off." He said as he slithered around another corner, always keeping the redhead insight, and waiting for just the right moment when she'd be alone.

"God why did she have to pick today to stop at every single shop and have a look see? Wait until I get her home, and she learns what a woman really is. It will be so much fun breaking her. I expect it will take quite a while, she is such a feisty thing, but the battle will be fun.

First it will be roses, candy, wine, a bit of courting to make her feel safe. Just like dad did to mom. I probably should have taken a couple of others first to practice on, but I do have what dad taught me, when mom and he were both still alive.

Lucky for me, dad left me quite a pretty penny, so I don't have to think about getting a stupid day job. Though it might have been easier to find my 'play toys' if I'd worked. Oh well, done is done and I should be picky with my first. The Devil knows I've waited long enough, after all first I had to play at the mourning thing for mom, and then for dad. But those years gave me time to plan, get the room ready. I mean who wants to use the old equipment dad used on mom. I want a bit of new stuff, and some of it had to be gotten quietly too."

CHAPTER TWO

I'm a pretty good-looking guy, especially if I hide the nature of my abilities. Perhaps I should court her first. Now how to meet her? There she's going into a jewelry shop. That's the place! I can go in and pretend to look around for something for my sister, (too bad that my aunt took my Rachael away from dad after mom died.) But I don't have to tell the redhead about that, and I can ask her opinion on a present, little will she know the presents will be for her. That should do the trick. It must be something that she'd love herself, and yes very expensive too, so she will know I have money. I'll use my Dubai Diamond Master Card, after all that one is by invitation only. Hehehe.

I expect I will have to take it all the way to marriage on this one, just like dad did. But perhaps I'll get a son out of her, before the fun starts. He thought walking into Tiffany's behind her.

Here comes the salesman, this will be quite easy, I think.

"My name is Roberts; may I be of service to you sir?"

"Possibly, though I think a woman's viewpoint might be more help to me." I said with just the right amount of haughty in my voice, not to much mind you. Just enough to make everyone take notice, especially the redhead, who turned around at my words, looking at me with those doe eyes of hers.

"I'm looking for something really special for my sister. It's her 18th birthday you see. It must be tasteful, but reek of her becoming a woman. She is very special and has been treated as such a child for much too long. I fear that has been wearing on her this last year."

"Follow me sir.' Said Mr. Roberts, as he led the way over to an assortment of pearl necklaces. 'Pearls are always a gift to give a girl who reaches her majority."

"I don't know. Pearls just don't speak to me.' I said as I noticed the redhead inching closer towards our counter. 'I'm sorry to bother you Miss, but I don't suppose you'd be kind enough to give me your opinion?"

"It would be my pleasure to help, my name is Rachael. I heard you say you are looking for a present for your sister."

"Hello Rachael, I'm Gerald and I'd really appreciate it. I'm not sure I'm keen on pearls, they seem so old fashioned to me. What is your opinion?"

"Gerald, I do think pearls can be just the right thing, but I personally prefer black pearls, they speak class and aren't so old fashioned as the traditional white ones."

"Rachael, what do you think of a simple diamond on a chain or maybe both? I know it would be spoiling her, but I haven't seen her for a few years, she lives with my aunt and uncle, since my parents died a few years ago, and I do miss her."

"Oh Gerald, I am so sorry about your folks." She said quietly, putting her hand on his arm for comfort."

"Thank you, it still hurts sometimes," he replied in the sincerest tone he knew. He visibly worked at pulling himself together, knowing all along that he had her now. *Thank the Devil that I've been practicing the so called (normal behaviors) all these years.* He thought. *But boy is it difficult to keep up the pretense that I have a normal human bone structure. I guess I should have spent more time in 'polite' society.*

Trying to hold the glee from his attitude, the salesman said. "Would you like to look at the black pearls or diamond necklaces first sir?"

"Since we are nearest the pearls let's look at them first and then move to the diamonds." Gerald said calmly, his hand still holding Racheal's.

"I like this one Racheal. Pointing at a large pearl necklace, what would you pick for yourself?"

"They are just a bit heavy looking to me Gerald, what do you think of these?" She said pointing to a daintier, but finer necklace, with a half carat white diamond in the middle of the clasp.

'Do you want to add these lovely black pearl earrings?" She said pointing to a pair of lovely pearl drop earrings.

"That's just the ticket. Put these in the back for us and point us in the direction of the diamonds please."

"Yes sir. They are over there.' He said pointing across the room. 'I'll be right over to help you."

Strolling across the room hand in hand, they headed toward the diamond necklaces.

"Gerald this is so much fun, picking out a birthday present for your sister. What is her name?"

"Funny thing is her name is Racheal too." Gerald said.

"REALLY?" What a coincidence."

"It is isn't it, I really was taken aback when you told me your name. I couldn't have been more shocked. She even has red hair, though she's not as tall as you are." He said looking admiringly at her.

He really is such a gentleman, and so very handsome too. Rachael thought. I feel so at ease with him, as if we'd known each other for years.

As they were looking over the diamonds, the salesman returned. "Did you have a particular type of diamond in mind sir?"

"Something tasteful, not to large, but not to small and of course it must be as perfect of a stone as you have in your store. I'd like it to be on a platinum chain and in a platinum setting too."

"Of course, sir." He said meekly leading the way. *Boy this guy must really have a bankroll, even bigger than I expected, and a great pick up artist too I might add.*

"What setting do you think I should get her Rachael?"

"Gerald, something a bit understated, I think. Not something flashy, but classy. If I were buying it, I'd get this setting.' She said pointing to a simple, understated setting. 'I believe this setting would draw the eye to the diamond, and not focus on the setting."

"Then that is what it will be.' Turning to the salesman, he said. 'How soon can you have it set?"

"I believe we could have it done and ready in about an hour. How many carats do you wish it to be?"

"Humm, do you think two carats is too much Rachael?"

"That is quite large, but I don't think to big. Especially if it was round."

"Do you have any perfect, registered diamonds of that size and shape?" Gerald asked the salesman.

"Yes sir. Is there anything else sir?"

"Yes, a pair of matching diamond studs. One must get the earrings to go with the necklace, mustn't one?" I expect you will want to write up the order now. Oh, I will take the black pearls and the black pearl drop earrings with me and come back for the diamonds."

"Yes sir, right this way. Jason, would you please wrap up the black pearls and earrings for the gentleman?"

"Right away Mr. Roberts."

CHAPTER THREE

I pulled out my Dubai First Master Card it's diamond flashing in the bright light on the counter, to a hiss of surprise from Mr. Roberts, and a hushed look of wonder from my soon to be bride. Mr. Roberts handed Gerald the blue tiffany box containing the black pearl necklace and earrings. We will see you in about an hour or so sir?"

"Yes Roberts. Oh, please put the diamond necklace in one of those silver Tiffany boxes and engrave the name Rachael on it please."

"Yes sir."

Turning to Rachael, Gerald said. "You've been so very kind to help me, and I feel as if we are already friends would you consent to having lunch or coffee with me, while I wait?"

"That would be lovely Gerald and I feel exactly the same about you." She replied as they walked out of the door.

"Would you mind going to Tinatello's?"

"I've never been there, but it sounds as if it would be wonderful, do you think we can get a table?"

"I'm sure we can." Gerald said in his most man about town voice.

I didn't expect this courting thing would be so much fun. I remember dad telling me it was, and that in the end, when the games began, it made it even more fun, because mom wasn't expecting them.

So, this week I court, and next week we marry. I should have her with child soon thereafter. Then the fun begins. A little gaslighting, just enough at first to make her think she is having memory problems. Then a bit more, not too much at least until after the child is weaned, and it better be a boy. But if not, I'll just drag it out a bit more till she has the boy I want too, and a girl would be fun too.

Just wait until she sees me in my natural element. I remember just how scared mother was when dad and I would creep up on her, nearly sliding under doors, and slithering across the floor. I do believe that is when mother really broke. But until then, I court...

I just can't believe my luck today, Rachael thought as they walked down the street toward the restaurant. *I think I could fall in love with this man.*

THE VOID
Marta Moran Bishop

CHAPTER ONE

Her long golden hair whipped in the breeze, flying into her face as it came loose from the black ribbon that had tied it. She watched the ribbon fly off, clinging to a tiny branch out of her reach. She couldn't climb further out; those branches were too slight to hold her small frame. The last dregs of light were sinking over the horizon as she settled herself as best, she could, wrapping her legs around the base of the branch and clinging to it with her slender arms.

Without the moon, tonight would be the darkest night of the year. So black even coal would seem bright in comparison. The stars which normally gave some light, however tiny that might be, were covered over by clouds. Each year there were the eleven dark moon nights and one that was the night of no moon, the moonless night. Helen disappeared near here last year on the moonless night. She had gone out late to fetch a bit of wood for their fire, and that was the last time anyone had ever seen her.

Since childhood, we both heard the warnings about this place on the no moon night, but how could we believe them? The villagers were all such an illiterate and superstitious lot, Altori mused. Why, they wouldn't even plant their crops in the fields below her.

Blackness descended. The sound of the hooting owls, calling crickets, and even the howling of the wolves stopped. Silence fell like a blanket over the air itself. Not a sound escaped— no whisper of leaves, no sound of wind—all was shrouded in nothingness till she thought she would scream. It pressed into her being, crowding her thoughts, stifling her ability to breathe, except in short, shallow gasps.

Closer and closer it came that terrible emptiness. The golden hairs on her arms stood up; her skin parched in the void. She could still feel her body, but she could not see. The closer the vacuum came, the less she could handle. Yet she held on and waited, for now, there was nothing she could do except wait, for any movement was impossible. Fear gripped her tightly in its arms. All too soon the silence was broken, not by the normal sounds of the night, but by chanting from below. It began slowly, shallowly, quietly, swelling, filling, and becoming the night.

Down below her on the prairie in the distance, lights danced with the harmony of the chants. Louder and louder they became, and the lights grew brighter and stronger until she could see something small dancing in the shadows of the flames. One creature became two, then three, until the plain below her filled, and she couldn't tell how many beings there were. Maybe, there was only one creature, and it had grown into one immense creature who had taken over the field. The chanting went on and on, the lights, and the creatures became the night itself; everything outside of them was nonexistent.

Altori watched and clung to the tree though she couldn't feel her arms or legs now. She held onto her thought of separateness, fearing she would lose herself as Helen must have if she surrendered to the night and the oblivion beyond the dancing, moving, chanting night. Then with an upsurge of the inundating presence below, it was gone, and the void pushed in on her again. She fought to hold onto her sanity once more. It must end soon, she thought. My name is Altori, I have a sister somewhere named Helen, and I live in the village on the other side of the forest. Her mind continued to shout these words to herself while she fought the oblivion, and abruptly that too was gone. She felt the roughness of the branch she was clinging to and heard the crickets singing the last of their night songs. A final wolf howled, and an owl hooted as the sky began to brighten.

Tangled in the leaves and the branches, her golden locks pulled with each movement of the wind. She shook with exhaustion, for with the disappearance of the void, so went the last of her strength. Still, she began the tedious job of removing the strands of her hair from the branches and leaves. Sometimes, she pulled in terror when she discovered a part of her hair had become one with the tree. Finally, sliding and nearly falling to the ground, sinking to her knees, she dropped and curled into a ball. She lay there for a few minutes unable to move.

I don't believe I can walk, she thought. Though I must get back to the village before dawn. No one must see me like this. Her brown dress was ripped, soiled with sap, sweat, and her fear; her hair was disheveled with twigs and leaves sticking in it. Her skin was entirely covered in scratches and soil. Lips parched, tongue swollen from thirst, she began to crawl. Pulling herself along until she managed with the help of a long branch, she got to her feet and staggered forward.

No thoughts went through her mind now, except two words: get home. Over and over they rolled around in her head--nothing else, just those two words—she hadn't the strength for anything else.

At last, her feet felt the dirt road of the village, and just as the cock crowed, she fell against the door of her small hut. Pulling herself into her home, shutting the door, she fell to her knees again, crawling to the water basin. She drank, lapping the water like a dog, quenching her thirst. Then ripping off what was left of her dress, she used a portion of it to wash.

Shivering in the crisp dawn air, not yet able to stand or light the stove, she pulled the raiments of her dress over her body and slept. Through the depth of her unconsciousness, she heard the pounding and banging on her door. It went on becoming louder and louder. It was insistent. Dragging herself to her knees, she yelled, "I'll be out as soon as I can. I'm not well today."

The banging stopped, and footsteps moved away from the door.

Still weak, Altori pushed herself to stand and staggered to the peg that held her only other, day dress. "Nothing can be done with that one," she said to herself as she looked at the rag lying on the floor in front of the door.

Turning, she made her way to the small table and slumped down on one of the rickety chairs beside it. In the middle of the table sat the day-old bread, dried out from sitting in the open air, and a block of cheese on a dish. It was to have been my supper, she mused as she gently pulled tiny pieces of the crumbly bread and stuffed it into her mouth.

Finally, able to hold a knife, she cut a small sliver of the cheese and ate that too. Still drained of energy but able to stand, she walked to the table by the bed, picked up her comb, and began to brush out her hair. When she had it as neat as possible, and the small bald spots were hidden— those spots that she had pulled out in chunks while trying to free it from the tree—she tied another ribbon around it. She hoped no one would notice. Usually, she felt invisible in the village and hoped today would be no different. No one must know she had been out in the void. No one must ever know. If Helen had been there, she could have talked about it with her, but after last night she feared that maybe the villagers were right, and she would never see Helen again.

The villagers had said Helen was gone for good, but Altori didn't believe them. She would have felt it if Helen was dead, and she didn't. Something was terribly wrong though, and somehow, she must find out what it was if she was ever to get Helen back. Today, she had her share of the village work to do. Even those who were invisible to the rest of the village had to work. The two of them usually went through the day unnoticed unless someone considered their workmanship shoddy or done incorrectly.

"I am an outsider here. Once when Helen was still here, I had someone I felt I belonged to. We were family. Now everything is empty," Altori spoke quietly to the walls and shuddered. "At least it isn't the void though."

Altori didn't know if she could go on feeling as if she didn't belong anywhere, yet where would she go? Would she fit in anywhere? If she left would she ever find Helen? She pondered these questions all day. Throughout her lunch break, sitting alone, as usual, she thought and wondered. What's the mystery? What was that thing or things down in the prairie last night? Her mind couldn't wrap itself around that question, and instead continued to shy away from any thought of that or of the void. "Think about tomorrow," it whispered to her.

CHAPTER TWO

This morning I was fortunate that Mistress Kyami was not around. Instead, Muralti doled out chores. Otherwise, things would have gone badly for me. Mistress Kyami was never easy, especially with those of us who were not her favorites, Altori thought. I must be more careful this afternoon. She likes her power and won't stay away long.

The laughter of the women at the other tables eating their lunches made the loneliness that much less bearable, but today it served its purpose. Head down, carefully keeping her scarf low across her head and partially hanging in her face, she hid the blackness of the bruises.

The morning had been hard enough, but Muralti was unused to handing out chores, and so she got light duty. She could barely stand. If she had spent the morning on her knees scrubbing the floor in the great hall, it would have been worse. That was one of the lowliest tasks given, and one that was reserved for those who irritated Mistress Kyami. The only one worse was cleaning the commodes. Altori thought I hope she is over her anger with me, or I will be assigned that this afternoon.

Stealing glances at the other women, she wondered again, where did Helen and I come from? How did we get to this village? I genuinely don't remember. We were both small and blonde, but the women of this village are tall, big boned, with the straightest, blackest hair one could ever have imagined. Where was Helen? Altori knew she wasn't dead. She felt her presence in her heart, and she was sure she would know if she died.

The world around her disappeared as she drifted into her memories. "Helen, what happened to you? You are covered in bruises, and I can see bald spots on your scalp. What are you doing on the floor? What happened to your dress? Oh my God, Helen, your face—your lips are swollen."

"Shush, speak quieter. Even though our hut is on the outskirts of the village, you never know who might be listening," Helen spoke in a hoarse whisper. "Please, Tori, bring me some water and a bit of bread. I am not well. I will tell you about it anon."

Altori took the pot of water off the hook over the small fire, dipped a cloth into it and quietly walked to her sister. "Let me wash you first, Helen—at least your poor face."

Helen only nodded. Unable to stand, she lay on the floor.

Altori placed a pillow under Helen's head and carefully washed her face and hands. They were covered in bruises black as night. Her golden hair was matted with twigs and leaves sticking out of it. She winced as Altori washed her face.

Helen put a hand up. "Water," she croaked. The look of pleading in her eyes made Altori move swiftly to fill a cup. She held it to Helen's mouth and watched her cracked lips part, and her swollen tongue nearly lapped the water. Altori's put her arm around her sister, propping her up while she drank. "More," she croaked as Altori ran and filled the cup again.

Startled out of her daydreams by the clanging bells that signaled the end of lunch, Altori pushed herself up, body aching. She looked down at the half-eaten piece of cheese and slice of bread. Hurriedly she picked them up, shoved them in the pocket of her dress, grabbed her cup of water, and scurried after the other women. She stood at the end of the line, waiting for her afternoon assignment. After she took the last sip of her water, she tucked the cup into the pack on her back and reached the head of the line.

Head lowered, she waited for Mistress Kyami and prayed she wouldn't notice the bruises that now covered her delicate hands. Reaching out, the woman grabbed one of her hands, and with a smug look on her face said, "Altori, if doing such a simple chore as peeling potatoes does this to your hands, you haven't been working hard enough." Still holding her hand roughly, she added, "I think this afternoon your task will be the commodes. Now make sure they are gleaming before you go home. After all, Monsieur and Madam are coming home tonight. It will be nice to have them back, won't it?"

"Yes, Mistress, it will," Altori said quietly, knowing if she were to say anything else it would go harder on her. With a hard slap on her back and a push that nearly knocked her off her feet, Kyami shoved Altori towards the row of outhouses. So strong was the stench, she could smell them fifty feet before she managed to drag her heavy feet to the door of the first.

"I can't do this," she said quietly to herself, nearly vomiting up the contents of her stomach. Pulling herself up she thought, I made it through the void, and I can do this. Just put one foot in front of the other and keep going. Spittle and urine covered the floor in front of the small wooden toilet. From the rack above her head, she lifted down a pail and brush. Retching, Altori heaved herself outside and managed to make it to the well without allowing herself to show weakness. Out of the corner of her eye, she could see Kyami laughing and joking with Annora. Both of them watched her with glee in their eyes.

Determination in her step now, Altori made her way back to the commodes. She knew no one had been assigned to clean them the entire time Monsieur and Madame had been gone. Kyami loved to wait until they were absolutely vile, and then her power became supreme.

How people can live like this is beyond me, Altori thought. Why don't they have the pride to clean up after themselves? Taking a cloth from her pocket, she tied it around her nose and commenced cleaning. This job will take me well past the usual quitting time, she thought. I expect that is why it has been given to me today. As I expected, Kyami has found a reason to make life even worse for me, being late is an unforgivable offense. Tomorrow is likely to be worse if anything can be worse than the commodes, she thought.

Dinner had come and gone, and a sliver of moon hung low in the sky when she finished her chores. As she stood outside the door of the last waiting for Kyami to inspect her work, she swayed with exhaustion. The piece of bread and cheese still in her pocket would have to do for her supper when she got home. A bit of water was left from her weekly allotment. She could wash and have a small glass. Luckily tomorrow they would dole out water. I hope they don't short me again this week, she thought.

Here she comes now; please, let it be satisfactory to her, Altori prayed and waited. She stood up as straight as she could while Kyami inspected each outhouse.

"Get in here, girl," Kyami shouted from the last of the outhouses.

"Yes, Mistress," Altori said quietly as she made her way into the last of the toilets.

"YOU SEE THAT? YOU MISSED A COBWEB!" Kyami screamed. "What kind of worker are you anyway? What kind of woman are you? I just don't see how you can be such a slacker all of the time."

"I'll get it right now, Mistress. I'm sorry. I should have seen it," Altori said, cringing from the berating. She had worked hours. Her hands were red and chapped. Her back ached, her throat parched, and her stomach empty.

"You do that right now. I'll watch, and tomorrow you will wash the floors in the great hall in the morning and clean these commodes again in the afternoon. I can't send you to the fields. You are too small and would make things harder for proper women—those who know how to do things correctly."

Altori cleaned the cobweb, her body swaying until finally, Kyami said, "You can use a bit of the water from the well to clean up before you go home. You stink. Make sure you have a clean dress on tomorrow." Kyami turned on her heel, but stopped, turned back, and with a smirk on her face said, "Don't use too much water, or it will be taken out of your weekly allotment."

Washing up at the well and using only a drop of water on her cloth, Altori's mind was blank. She was much too tired to do anything except wobble home afterward.

She opened her door and staggered in, pulling the soiled dress off. She noticed her bruises were worse and remembered. "My God, Helen, you look worse today. I will cover for you again, but I fear soon it will become impossible to do so."

"I'm sorry, Altori," Helen said while lying on the small bed in the corner. Her bruised face was now full of large welts. "I wish I could get up, but I can't. I don't want to make it harder for you, but please, before you go put some of that cooling cream on my back. It feels as if it is on fire."

Altori tiptoed over to her sister with the jar of cream in her hand. Carefully she turned Helen over and moved the nightdress away from her back. Altori almost gagged. The black bruises had become tremendously huge lumps, which oozed a green-tinged fluid. It smelled awful. With a tender, feather-like touch, she smeared the cream over Helen's back. "You may need a doctor, Helen. These look terrible. They are worse than yesterday."

"We can't, Tori, she replied. "They would know I was in the void. They might put me in 'the box' for fear someone would catch something from me. I'd die in the box, Tori. Do what you can. I will be okay."

"I'll make sure you are safe, Helen, but I am worried. It has been three months now, and each day you look worse."

The memories faded as she cleaned her dress and hung it on the peg. Looking at Helen's dress on the other peg, she murmured to herself, "I will have to wear that tomorrow. My own won't be dry, and the other I must patch."

CHAPTER THREE

Still wobbly from the night before, Altori pulled open the door of her small hut. I must get through today, she thought. Somehow, I must, and I must find a way to earn enough to afford the cloth to make another dress. I feel that I am giving up on Helen by wearing her dress. Please, don't let them notice all these bruises. They are worse today, she thought just before Mistress Kyami came into view.

"You're late! What is wrong with you? Why are you all bruised?" She said, her voice almost a scream.

"I am sorry, Mistress Kyami. I fell last night. I didn't feel well and tripped over a chair in the dark," Altori said with her head lowered. She knew better than to meet the head mistress's eyes. She had once a few years ago and felt the lash for it. Besides, she didn't want her to see she wasn't telling the complete truth.

"Well don't let it slow you up today, or there will be hell to pay. We can't afford slackers in this village." She loved to punish Altori any and every chance she could.

"Thank you, Mistress Kyami," she said as she turned onto the path that leads to the great hall. She knew scrubbing the floors on her hands and knees would be brutal. Her body quaked with hunger, thirst, and exhaustion. She didn't turn to watch the look of joy she knew was on the mistress's face. It was there, and she knew it. I won't give you the satisfaction of knowing how much this will hurt, she thought, moving as quickly as she was able.

Her steps slowed a bit as soon as she was out of Kyami's sight. I will get through this, she thought as she took the pail and brush from the closet. She walked into the great hall.

Annora stopped working and moved toward Altori, momentarily looking her over, before giving her a small shove. "You are not to hold us up today. We don't care if you fall over later, but there is work to do today." She turned and with a chortle went back toward the other women. "She's not worth her weight, but she will pull it and more today," she told them as they all looked at Altori. They laughed and went back to their work.

Their job was dusting and cleaning the silver, a light task, one Altori wished she had, she thought as she filled her bucket and began scrubbing the floors. At least I'll be left alone. Scrubbing floors can be a tedious job, she thought as she sunk back into her memories.

"Helen, where are you? Oh my God!" She nearly screamed as she saw the pile of hair lying on the pillow. She spied a small crumpled piece of paper on the table. Altori picked it up and read it.

Dearest Tori,

I can't continue to make you try to cover for me. Physically I am stronger, but my skin is getting worse. Today most of my hair fell out. I'm a horror now and am going to slip away and hide till this passes. I might have to see if I can find the void again. Maybe that will heal me? Regardless, I know this is the only way. Give Mistress Kyami the note I wrote to her. It will help ease your burden while I'm gone. It is sealed, so I will tell you that it says I am going to visit family for a bit. She will not believe it and will probably think I've run away or am dead, but it will help you. Lastly, the third note is a phony note to you saying much the same as her note. Let her read that one too. It will help keep you above suspicion. Tori, I love you. We will see each other soon. It may not be for a year or two, but we will see each other. You will know in your heart if something happens to change that. Until then, stay safe.

Much love,

Helen

She fell to the floor sobbing. That night and every night since she cried. Still, she knew Helen was somewhere safe. But, where?

Waking from her trance, Altori realized she had finished the great hall. She still had to wax the floor but would be able to finish that before the lunch bell rang. Looking down at her hands she saw her skin was beginning to show signs of the welts that preceded the green puss. She had no one to cover for her. What would she do? She knew if someone saw this, she would be put in the box, just as Helen had feared a year ago would happen to her. She would die in the box, yet where else could she go? How would she hide these horrid changes that were taking over her body? It was a year till the next night of no moon. She must make it through today. At least the green puss took a month or two to manifest if it followed the same pattern as with Helen. Somehow, tonight she must figure out what she would do over the next few months. She was frightened.

CHAPTER FOUR

Her small hand covered her mouth to stifle the scream as she pulled herself up. Braced against the wall, she looked down at the massive amount of golden hair covering her pillow. Tears ran down her face and stung as she cried. She reached up to touch her head and felt the small patches of hair that still clung to her scalp, but most of her hair lay on the pillow. "How will I hide this? Use your brain, Altori." She cried silently. "Eat. It will give you a bit of strength."

Slowly, she placed her feet on the floor, wincing with the pain. Her skin was now a mass of welts and bruises. One foot in front of the other, she thought, hobbling, to the unfinished coffee colored table. On top of it sat a loaf of stale bread, a wedge of cheese, one side of it covered in a thin layer of blue mold, and a bowl full of overripe apples left over from the last picking. She picked up her only knife, cut a wedge of cheese, a slice of bread, and pared the apple. After placing them on a cream-colored plate, she sat. The rungs of the straight-backed chair dug into her back and caused her to smother another yelp. Instead, she placed her elbows on the table and held herself away from the back of the chair as she ate her meal.

After a few bites and a sip of cold water, Altori's mind began to clear. With the fog of sleep gone, she started to make her plans. "I'll use some of the cream I make especially for the Mistress to cover the dark circles under her eyes on my welts. I believe I can braid the hair and sew it into my work cap," she murmured aloud, glancing at the hair that nearly hid her pillow. It was difficult to look at, and she feared to look in the mirror, which stood in the corner of the room. That mirror had remained covered since before Helen left. Altori hadn't paid attention to how she looked after Helen was gone, and Helen hadn't wanted to look upon the horror that she had become after her trip into the void.

"Whatever possessed me to go into the void anyway?" Altori mused as she carefully applied the cream on her welts. "If I can keep them out of the water, I believe it will work. Where are those gloves? I will need them today."

Carefully she placed the small brown work hat on her head and tied the ribbons tightly under her chin. Prudently, she eyed herself in the mirror. She made sure the braids she had sewn into the hat appeared to be her hair and not a part of the cap. "It certainly helps that I never wore bangs, or I would have the devil's own time making it look like my hair," she muttered to herself. "Good. I believe it works, and my bald head doesn't show."

After she applied a bit of the cream to the bruises on her face and hands, she muttered, "Well, I think if I keep my head down, no one will notice." She closed the door behind herself and walked down the path to the great house to wash and polish the floors.

The bells from the church rang out so loudly she thought she would go deaf. I wonder what is going on, she thought, as she trotted closer to the large group of villagers who stood in front of the great house. Quickly making her way closer, she heard the crier calling everyone to order.

"Hear, hear!" he yelled to quiet everyone down. "The master will be back soon. His runner came in a few minutes ago. He will tell us all the news. Until then, stand quietly."

A hush fell over the crowd, though a bit of jostling went on as people vied for a better position. Standing away from the group but still near enough to see, Altori waited. The shelter of a large oak tree kept the glare of the morning sun out of her eyes, which had grown sensitive to light. The wait wasn't long.

The master road up on his bay horse. His horse was lathered in sweat, and the master's gray silk was suit stained with his perspiration. His black leather boots had lost their shine. His hat had gone somewhere in his flight home.

A groomsman took the sweating bay, tied it to the rail, and melted into the crowd as the master climbed the stairs to the wide porch that wrapped around the great house. For a moment, he took his wife in his arms, held her and whispered something in her ear before turning. His large brown hands clasped the railing of the porch. His grip was so tight on the rail his knuckles turned white. The crowd was silent now. The crier stepped back behind the mistress, and the master looked up.

"We all know the void happens on the night of no moon. It is true that this is a dangerous time for us all, and we must prepare the village for this night. No one must be out; no window must be uncovered. All animals, livestock, and family pets must be sheltered in their barn with the hatches battened down. No glimpse of the sky, the earth, or the air must reach anything that has blood running through its veins. We also know that the night of no moon only happens once every year. What we didn't know is that every thousand years, there are four no moon nights."

The air filled with cries of horror from the crowd.

"Shush, shush," the crier yelled. "The master is still talking."

"This year is the year of four no moon nights, and because of this, there will be four voids. It will be a hard year. No one must waste a minute on any project that does not involve putting aside food, clothing, water, or other stores. Each able-bodied man must make sure all roofs, walls, doors, and windows are tight. We must be ready. Unfortunately, we have only one day to do it in. The astronomers were clear about this." He grasped the hand of his wife while they both took a child in their other arm.

"Master, how can this be?" the tall, dark, large-nosed man asked loudly.

"Why weren't we told before?" someone else in the crowd yelled.

The master put his little boy down, turned back around to the crowd, held up one hand and said, "The histories were lost in a fire a hundred years ago. Since then the astronomers have been working nonstop to read the signs. No one wanted to believe this was the year. No one wanted to believe this horror would happen in our lifetimes. However, it is true. There is no question of it, and everything has been checked in every way possible."

A groan went up from the crowd. Men were holding their wives close to their chests. A few of the women had swooned.

"My friends and neighbors, I wish this was not true, but it is. The void is coming, and because it is so near the last, it will be worse. We must make ready. Stay here while I speak to the foremen and women so chores can be assigned correctly. There will be no washing of floors. Each of you must clean up after yourself as best you can in the commodes and the kitchens."

A shriek came from the crowd as another woman fainted. Her family pulled her to her feet and braced her body against theirs.

"All must be ready. Take a short rest, my friends, while I speak to the foremen," the master said as he turned and went into the great house.

He was followed by five men and five women, all of them large, brown, and brawny. None of the foremen could be called small or delicate. Each wore a red kerchief around their neck and a large straw hat upon their head.

The crowd sat on the ground. Some were whispering to each other, while others sobbed loudly.

Altori sat in the shelter of the tree and waited. Maybe, I can go back into the void, she thought. I might die, or I might heal. Perhaps I will find Helen or learn what those lights are in the void.

Whatever I find, I must go, for I will not last here in this village the way I am now.

CHAPTER FIVE

The air was thick with angst. It seemed as if the very trees around the village were bursting with the need to scream and cry. Far off in the distance could be heard the noise of hammers and saws coming from the next village. Yet no one moved. Each man, woman, and child sat staring at the door to the great house. All were waiting. Even those holding small children waited.

Just before the door opened to the great house, a baby cried, and a dog barked. Then a hush fell over the crowd as the foremen and women poured forth. Each walked as if the weight of the world lay on their shoulders. As one, their heads rose, and they stood staring at the sea of faces. For a moment no one spoke. This group of men and women appeared unable to talk or even step off the porch of the great house.

Finally, the master came out of the house, his arms around his wife. Her finery was gone, and she wore a simple brown dress similar to those of every other woman who lived in the village. Her hair was tied up under a worker's cap. The master had also changed. His smart gray suit had been replaced with a pair of brown pants tied at the waist and a rough white shirt tucked into the pants. On his head, he wore a wide-brimmed straw hat, and his black leather boots had been replaced with the rugged leather footwear of the villagers.

Loudly the gong rang, and the crier called everyone to order. Each foreman and forewoman walked down the stairs and moved into line in front of the villagers. They almost formed a wall with their bodies. Each man, woman, and child was assigned a place in line behind one of the foremen. Even the women with babies were hustled into one of the lines.

The master called out loudly, "Take your children to your mistress. It will be her job to watch over them as we prepare. You will see me walk among you as you complete the tasks set for you. Everything I tell you must be remembered."

Altori stood. Before she was called, she moved forward and joined the sea of brown. Among these people there was no shoving or pushing, just a steady movement as each person moved forward. As tasks were assigned, the one in the front left to collect their tools. I have lived in this village thirty years now, she mused, though I know not how old I am. I don't believe I know the name of one single man, woman, or child, except for my direct forewoman. My first memories are of being an outcast, not accepted into the fold, or allowed to intermingle with anyone. It's no wonder I have no friends. It's good that I don't know anyone, for there's less chance they will notice my affliction.

The sweat of fear prevailed, so strong that Altori could barely hold her breakfast down. It seemed her sense of smell had increased along with the welts, bruises, and loss of hair. She wondered what other changes would happen. Helen didn't stay in the village long enough for her to know. Where did she go? It had been over a year now and not a word from her. Now no one asked about her, which was good, because she had no answers for them.

Soon she faced Mistress Kyami. Head down, she waited for her fate for the next few days and prayed it would be a task she could handle in her present condition. Kyami was so intent on the list in her hands, she never looked up at Altori. Instead, she quietly announced, "Because you are such a small thing, I cannot assign you to many tasks that we could use an extra hand with. I expect the most valuable thing you can do is to spend the next few days in the kitchens canning and putting aside the food that will be brought in from the fields, so the master can dole it out to the households when the time arrives. Is your shanty shielded?"

"Yes, Mistress. I have kept it up to date on all repairs."

"Good, for there would be no time to send someone to seal your cabin, and no other person in this village has room for the likes of you. Now off with you."

As Altori stepped out of line, she heard the snickers of those still left. It was sad really. Sometimes she wondered if anyone there would notice her gone. Probably the first day or so when she didn't come for her scheduled chores.

Up above the village, large black birds flew, the wind whipped the branches of the trees, and sounds of hammers and saws filled the air. Around her, the world narrowed into swirls of the large, dark-haired, brown clothed men and women as they moved through their chores. The volley of noise and flurry bombarded her senses as she made her way to the kitchen of the great house.

"Lord, it is unseasonably hot today," cried the head cook. "You're that girl that Kyami told me about, the useless one, aren't you? Well, I'm going to tell you, there will be no slacking in here. You will pull your weight or get whipped and get nothing for yourself to take you through the void for the next two nights. You have a name girl?"

"Altori," she said softly.

"Just call me Cook. That's what everyone calls me. It's been so long since I've been called anything else, I barely remember if I have another name," she said dryly. "No matter. You sure are an insignificant little thing, aren't you? Do you know anything about canning or putting stores up?"

"I make the cream for the mistress and do all my own canning," Altori answered.

"Alright then. You know a bit more than some they're sending me today." She looked Altori up and down. "Maybe you'll be of use if you don't slack off."

Terrified that Cook would look too closely and see the welts on her hands and face, or that her hair was not really a part of her head, Altori quickly said, "Would you like me to peel and pare the fruit and vegetables as they come in?"

"Yes, that would be good," Cook said and turned to the next woman in line to give her instructions.

Pulling on her gloves, Altori thought, I am truly blessed today. I can work far enough away from the others, and if I keep my head down and my hands out of the water, it's possible with all of the urgency today that no one will notice me—at least as long as I work quickly and keep out of the way.

"Helen are you out there? Will I find you at midnight when the void comes, or will I die? And if I die, will I find you then?" she pondered silently as she peeled and pared, dropping each vegetable in its bowl as she finished with it. "If I go into the void tonight, and it is worse than the first, can I live through it? I barely made it through the last. I wonder what would have happened if I had been in the field below and not up in the tree. Would it have been so bad? Something goes into that field during the void. What is it? It frightens me. Would it eat me alive? Whatever it is down there, is it as bad as the nothingness that presses in on one outside of that field? Is that vacuum down in the field too? If so, how does that entity—or is it many beings—exist in the vacuity? What is it?" Altori thought as basket after basket of fruits and vegetables were placed in front of her.

The humidity filled the room with a haze as the afternoon became evening. With the extreme heat of the day, the many pans of water boiling for the canning, and the smoker working overtime to make enough bacon and jerky to last the few hundred people that made up the village through the void and its aftermath. Altori could barely even see the hands of the women who picked up her peeled vegetables and those who dropped off more baskets for her to peel and pare. Eventually, the stacks began to dwindle. Now the largest of the farm women and men were carrying in huge baskets of potatoes, onions, and garlic. These were piled high in the cellar under the kitchens.

Finally, cook yelled, "Roundup, leave your pans, and go help bring the animals into the barns. Don't worry about the clean-up. We'll do that after the void has passed."

Quickly each woman dropped her knife, spoon, ladle, or whatever tool she'd been working with and rushed to the door. Altori reeled as she stood. No one had even stopped for a lunch break, and she was weak from hunger and rising nausea brought on by her brutal malady. She steadied herself, picked up a carrot laying by itself on the large butcher block table, and stuck it into the pocket of her dress. Then she grabbed a container of water and walked out the door. She tried to stay as steady as possible so as not to call attention to herself and made her way to the fields and paddocks. At the fence, each person gathered a rope and a short crop in their hands and made their way into the meadow.

Clouds hung low in the sky and seemed to hurry night on. They swirled and spun now, as the birds flew squawking and shrieking around the fields and village. Each villager who could walk, even the smallest of children, carried or led an animal. Three small boys carried baby goats. The boys' backs nearly bent as they hurried to the barns. Altori watched a group of little girls probably not more than four or five clutch chickens and kittens in their arms as they followed the boys.

The very atmosphere felt thicker. Sulfur, black smoke from the kitchen chimneys, sawdust from the cutting of both firewood and wood to seal the windows and doors, hung in the air. The trees appeared to be ready to walk forward, and the dirt of the path, even packed down as it was, began to whirl as the last of the horses, cows, sheep, goats, and chickens were led into the barn.

The night was coming quickly, much faster than was normal for this time of year, even here in this valley between the hills. Altori couldn't remember a void that had caused the night to fall this rapidly. Children were crying, and women were screaming as the last of the barn doors were closed.

GONG … GONG … GONG … The crier hit the brass bell on the great house porch calling everyone to order.

"Line up," the master yelled at the top of his voice. "LINE UP to get your supplies. QUICKLY NOW! If you don't hurry, you will not be in your homes on time. The void is coming early, make haste everyone."

In front of the kitchen, the master and mistress stood alongside the cook, foremen, and forewomen. Behind each stood baskets of food, firewood, and water. Rapidly, nearly in a frenzy, each villager took their baskets. Even the young children carried water or food. Some held their smaller brothers or sisters in their arms or carried a new baby.

Altori stood waiting near the end of the line. Her skin was too raw now to take a chance of someone touching her.

CHAPTER SIX

It was almost entirely dark when she fell through her doorway. The basket that held a few pieces of firewood, a couple of bottles of water, a loaf of bread, a block of cheese, a few tomatoes and potatoes, and the rare piece of beef jerky and slab of bacon flew from her hands. The vegetables and potatoes rolled across the floor. Crawling forward, she pushed the door closed with her foot.

The darkness was complete. Not a single speck of light came through her door or windows. Luckily since her illness, she had taken to covering the windows, so that didn't need to be done now. Out of her pocket, she pulled the carrot, wiped lint from it, and bit down into it. Lying on the floor, she chewed the carrot and fumbled herself into a sitting position.

First, food and water, she thought. Do I make a fire? Am I going back into the void? If so, I will need to hurry, for I must be in that field before it hits. Once midnight comes there would be no possibility of walking or even crawling—not in the void. If I don't leave soon, it will be too difficult anyway. What's happening outside now is nearly as bad as the void was when I went into it the last time.

With a deftness previously unknown to Altori, she began to find each item and place them back into the basket. "I don't understand," she thought. "I'm beginning to be able to see, and it is pitch black in here. I can almost hear the sound of the wood lying on the floor, and I can see the potatoes, tomatoes, cheese, and bread." She turned, and her hand fell on a greasy slab of bacon. It reeked, making her gag. The smell of the meat filled her nostrils until she thought she couldn't breathe. Carefully she picked up the bacon and jerky packed inside the cheesecloth, opened the door, and tossed them both out, throwing them as far from her home as her small, tired arms could manage.

Exhausted, lying on the floor, food, and firewood in the basket beside her, she slept a while, only to wake to the sound of the wind picking up through her open door. Her hand reached out and touched one of her containers of water and pulled it closer. She pushed herself into a sitting position. With both hands around the water bottle to keep them from shaking, she brought it to her lips and drank deeply. Some of it splashed down the front of her dress and left trails of slime from soil and sweat mixed with the dirt of the floor.

On the floor next to her lay her cap and braids. Somehow in her sleep, she must have pulled it off her head. She ran one tiny hand over her head and restrained herself from screaming. She was completely bald. The few strands of hair she had that morning were lying in her hat or on the floor next to where she had slept.

Outside the wind howled, the leaves swirled into what appeared to be miniature tornadoes. It must be getting close to midnight, Altori thought as she pulled herself to her feet and shut the door. "What I must do now to make myself ready can't be seen. Even though I know that not one man, woman, or child is outside now, I still must be careful," she said quietly.

CHAPTER SEVEN

The darker it becomes, the stronger I feel, she thought as she walked over to the far wall. Behind the mirror was a small black box tucked into the corner. It's been many years since I've even thought about this box, she mused, looking down on it.

She squatted down and pulled it near her. At the first touch, her memories flooded through her. "This is my legacy!" Altori croaked, afraid to even speak the words.

"Come along, Tori," Helen said, carrying the black box in both hands as they walked down the dirt path into the village.

Along each side of the path sat a house, most without windows. In others, the windows were boarded up. No trees lined the way, not a dog barked, nor could the sound of children playing be heard in the village. The houses, brown and squat, appeared to hunker down as if afraid. Off in the distance stood a grand house with white columns that held the roof over the long porch, which ran the length of the house. Altori stood there transfixed.

"I said, come along, Tori. We can't stand in the street like this. It isn't safe, nor is it polite," Helen added.

"Helen, where are we going?" Tori squeaked; her high, childish voice filled the air around them.

"Shush now. I'll show you. Just a little further and right now we mustn't be seen."

On the other side of the enormous house, they could see men, women, and children, in the field far off in the distance. "What are the people doing, Helen?"

"I expect they are working the fields."

"I'm hungry and tired. Mightn't we sit for a moment?"

"Soon little one. We must get to our new home first and put the box away. No one must see the box, Tori."

"Why? What's in the box?"

"A bit of magic along with our legacy, little sister. Come along, quickly now."

Toward the outskirts of the town sat a little shack hidden from view behind a barrier of poplar trees. Altori's small legs could barely carry her now, and she stumbled every now and then.

The box in Helen's arms appeared to grow larger each time Altori looked at it. With care, Helen placed it on the stoop in front of the small shanty and opened the door, letting a musty dead smell fill their nostrils. "It will need a might of cleaning, I think," Helen stated, smiling down at the little girl, thumb in her mouth, standing next to her.

Once more picking up the box, her arms shaking with exhaustion, Helen turned to Altori and said, "After you, little one."

Altori shook the cobwebs of memories from her mind as she opened the box. Lying on top sat a large black book covered in a layer of dust. Altori traced a finger along the gold dragon that was etched into the cover. She lifted the box and placed it on the floor.

"Tori, wash your face and hands, and we can eat."

"Helen, where are Momma and Papa?" Altori asked.

"I don't know, Tori. The winds and dark separated us from them. We will need to stay here a while until we figure out how to get home."

"Where is here?" Altori asked as she sat down at the table and put a piece of cheese in her mouth.

"I don't know that either. We mustn't talk about any of this now. Not until we figure it out. I fear it will be a bit difficult getting settled in this village. Hopefully, we won't be here long. Eat now. Tomorrow we will see what we can do to survive in this village and gain a measure of acceptance."

CHAPTER EIGHT

Altori's hands lifted the soft black velvet cloth out of the box and carefully placed it next to the book. Next, she took out the one silver candlestick, a silver vial of scented oil, and a willow branch. Each piece she picked up and laid out on the table. First, she covered the table with the cloth, then she placed the candle and candlestick, book, and willow branch on the fabric.

I must move cautiously, but quickly now, she thought. She walked over to her basin, poured a small amount of water into it, and then took the vial and tipped three drops of oil into the water. She walked back to the table. With a gentle caress, she wiped the dust from the book and opened it. As if a small wind rushed through the room, the pages turned faster and faster until stopping, as if the book itself knew what she needed. Looking down, her hands picked up a tiny sliver of paper with Helen's handwriting on it. As she read it, she moved back to the basin. The darkness completely saturated the room, but still, she could see.

Hurriedly, she removed the brown dress and stockings that had been her clothing and covered her from head to toe for many years now. She picked up a strip of white cloth she had saved, dipped it into the water, and began to wash. With each breath she took, she recited, "I cleanse myself of the dirt of the road. I clear my heart of the dust of the village. I purify my soul from the horrors of all ill thoughts, both mine and those of others." Finally, she plunged her bald head and face into the basin of scented water. Head dripping, she said, "My mind is unblemished by the dangers in the village and those in the void."

Still dripping wet, she walked to the table and waved her hand over the candle in the holder. From somewhere deep inside, from a place she had never known existed, a power came rushing forth, and a tiny flame rose on the candle. Again, she recited, "I cleanse myself of the dirt of the road. I clear my heart of the dust of the village. I purify my soul of the horrors brought by ill thoughts, both mine and those of others. My mind and body are unblemished by the dangers in the village and those in the void."

For a moment she stood there, head bowed, and then she carefully packed each item back into the black box. As she sealed it, she chanted, "You will follow me unseen. Not a beast of the forest or a human of the village will see you. Like a feather, you will float on the wind behind me."

Her white skin glistened from her cleansing. Her mind was still from the spell. Naked she walked to the door, flung it open, and went into the night, leaving behind the clothes of the village and the basket of food, firewood, and water still on the floor. Her blonde hair still sewn into the little worker's cap laying in the shadow of the stoop.

Lightly her feet covered the distance. Almost flying now, dancing with the wind that whipped between the trees, she raced on. She could feel the void coming, the pressure building in that unearthly way. "I will make it," she screamed as she ran forward, pushing through the building pressure of the coming void and into the pastureland below the village. Farther and farther she ran until she stood in the center of the ring of stones, which were placed there eons ago and then forgotten.

Around her whirled the winds, yet at the center it was calm. Far off she heard the screams of those blooded creatures that were out in the void, but not in its center. She knew what they felt as the nothingness took over. The black hole of the void swirled around the perimeter of the field.

The chanting began as before, only more evident now. "We cleanse ourselves of the dust of the road. We clear our hearts of all old hurts. We purify our souls as we seek our lost ones. Our bodies and minds are unblemished. Freely we enter this world. We seek no harm. We seek our own."

One by one the lighted candles ignited around her, enveloping her in the sweet scents of clean earth, flowers, and perfumes. Overhead she saw the clear skies and bold, bright stars, covering the black sky inside the ring of fire that swelled and bloomed around her. The chanting rose as it moved closer to her, embracing her in the warmth of the home she barely remembered. Before her stood Helen, long blonde hair whipping in the balmy breeze of the tropical night. Arms open she said, "Come along, Tori. Come home."

Helen stood with her arms cradling her sister as the circle of light tightened. The chanting rose, and as one, Altori and Helen joined in. The winds rushed around the field, churning a funnel. Nothing outside of the circle existed. All life was in this small circle of rocks. All else was the void. As the chanting grew louder, the people moved closer, and the whirlwind in the black hole took them home. "We seek no harm. We seek our own."